THE ENCHANTED CHRISTMAS

Adapted by Diane Muldrow
Illustrated by Alan Nowell

Based on Disney's *Beauty and the Beast: The Enchanted Christmas* produced by Walt Disney Television Animation. Written by Flip Kobler & Cindy Marcus and Bill Motz & Bob Roth.

 **A GOLDEN BOOK • NEW YORK**

Golden Books Publishing Company, Inc., New York, New York 10106

It was Christmastime and the Prince's castle looked like a fairyland with garlands, evergreens, and the biggest Christmas tree young Chip had ever seen!

"It's good to see the boy having a proper Christmas!" Lumiere said as he watched Chip play among the gifts. "Certainly not like last year!"

"Yes," agreed Cogsworth. "This is much more agreeable!"

"Please tell the story, Mama! About last Christmas?" Chip pleaded.

So Mrs. Potts settled into a chair and began, "Well, let's see . . . Belle had been the Master's guest for a little while, and we all hoped that she would be the one to break the spell. There was no time to waste, so somehow we got them to ice-skate together the day before Christmas."

The servants watched as Belle taught the Beast how to
ice-skate on the pond. Everyone was happy . . . everyone, that
is, except Forte, the pipe organ. For if Belle and the Beast fell
in love, the spell cast over the whole castle would be broken,
and everyone would become human again. Then the Beast
would no longer need the gloomy music Forte liked to play.

"Fife, what's that merriment I hear outside the window?" asked Forte.

"Oh," replied the little piccolo, "the Master is skating with Belle."

"Belle?" cried Forte. "That will never do! Fife, see to it that this blossoming love wilts on the stem. Go stop them now!"

"Yes, Maestro Forte!" said Fife, bounding away.

"Pardon me . . . coming through . . . TWEET!"
announced Fife, pushing his way through the crowd. He
slid onto the ice, then grabbed the Beast's cape and
caused him and Belle to fall into a snowbank.

"Look! I made a Christmas angel," Belle cried.

The Beast stood and stared at his own hideous shape in the snow.
"This is no angel. It's the shadow of a . . . monster!" he roared.
Then he stormed away. "I hate Christmas!"

Fife was pleased. "Oh, Forte will be so proud of me!" he said
to himself.

Belle decided that the Beast needed some Christmas cheer, even though Cogsworth warned her that the Master had forbidden Christmas. "He doesn't wish to be reminded of the Christmas when the castle was put under the curse," he explained.

But Lumiere and Mrs. Potts agreed with Belle, so up to the dusty attic they went.

There, among the crates and broken furniture, stood a pretty Christmas angel. "Ah, Lumiere!" the angel cried happily.

"This is Angelique, the castle decorator," Lumiere proudly announced. "Cherie, we're planning the greatest celebration ever! And we need your help!"

But Angelique shook her head and said sadly, "No, no. I refuse to hope for Christmas anymore. I will not be disappointed again!"

Later that day, the Beast found a present from Belle marked DO NOT OPEN UNTIL CHRISTMAS.

"I said no Christmas presents!" he shouted. But the Beast touched the gift and smiled, then went to tell Forte to stop playing his gloomy music.

"Sorry, old friend, but I don't feel gloomy anymore," explained the Beast. "I want you to compose a song. It's a present for . . . Belle. And make it a happy song!"

Forte frowned. After the Master left the room, Forte dreamed up a plan that would get Belle out of the castle—for good.

"These trees don't look very Christmasy," Belle told Chip as they rode through the eerie Black Forest. Forte had told her that the tree was the Beast's favorite part of Christmas, and that the Black Forest was the perfect place to get one.

Back at the castle, everyone was frantically searching for Belle.
"She must have gone all the way into the Black Forest!" cried
Lumiere as he spotted the tracks in the snow.

"What will we tell the Master?" Cogsworth cried. "He's been
looking for Belle! We must hurry and find her!"

Meanwhile, in Forte's chamber, the Beast could no longer wait for Belle. He grabbed the magic mirror and shouted, "Show me the girl!"

There in the reflection he saw Belle riding away in the sleigh.

"I'll bring her back!" shouted the Beast.

Forte saw his chance. "No, Master," he said quickly. "She's abandoned you!"

The Black Forest was dark as Fife secretly followed Belle and Chip.

As Belle and Chip began to tow their tree home, Fife tried to unhitch Phillipe the horse from the sleigh and accidentally revealed himself. "Whoa!" Fife cried.

Fife's high-pitched tooting sound startled Phillipe. He bolted and broke loose from the sleigh—causing Chip to fall into the icy water!

Belle jumped in and saved Chip, but the icy currents were too much for her. Suddenly, a loud roar echoed through the forest. It was the Beast! He dove deep into the water and emerged with Belle, then carried her back to the castle as the others followed.

"What have I done?" cried Fife. "It's all my fault. I never should have listened to that Forte. He put me up to all of this!"

The Beast took Belle to the dungeon.
"You said you'd never leave," he growled.
"I wasn't trying to leave. I just wanted
to make you happy," sobbed Belle.
"You broke your word," shouted the
Beast. "And for that, you'll stay here
forever!" He stormed up the stairs and
Belle felt completely alone.
"Bong . . . bong . . . bong . . ."
Somewhere in the silent castle,
a clock struck midnight.
Christmas had come.

The enchanted objects crept down to visit Belle.
Angelique stepped forward. "I told you that Christmas was a
hopeless folly!" Then her face softened as she said, "But I
was wrong. We must have Christmas!" She began to sing a
sweet Christmas song. Everyone joined in, even Belle.

   Upstairs in Forte's chamber, the Beast finally opened Belle's gift—a book about a cold-hearted prince who discovered the warmth and joy of friends, and of Christmas. After reading it, he sighed and said, "Maybe there is still hope for me."

   As the Beast left the room, Forte cried desperately, "Master! Come back! Belle is not your friend—I am!" But the Master was gone.

Belle and the others were startled when the Beast appeared in the middle of their celebration. He stood before Belle and gazed into her eyes.

"Belle, can you forgive me?" he asked.

"Of course," replied Belle gently. "Merry Christmas."

Everyone was happy, except Forte. He began to play a horrible song that blasted through the castle and shook the walls. Dust flew everywhere as the ceiling began to crumble!

The floor of the dungeon cracked open between Belle and the Beast.

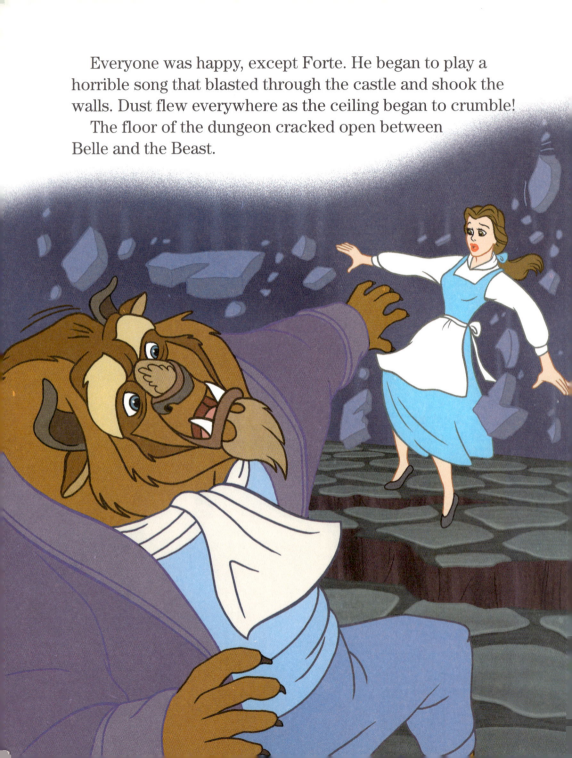

The Beast bounded up to Forte's chamber while Belle and the others followed.

"Forte! Enough!" he shouted. He tore the keyboard from the organ. The music soared, then stopped. Forte was so angry that he ripped himself from the wall with all his might and smashed to the floor.

All was silent. Finally the Beast said, "What are we standing around for? Let's give Belle the Christmas she's always wanted!"

And what a Christmas it was. The Beast and Belle laughed and danced together. Angelique's beautiful decorating and the scrumptious food were enjoyed by one and all.

"And that's when Belle and the Beast began to fall in love. Thank goodness!" said Mrs. Potts. "Soon the spell was broken and we all became human and happy . . . again."